For Neha and Suzanna

Thanks to the Home-Start Renfrewshire family group: Julie Alexander, Stephanie Barn,
Joanne Blair, Lynne Ewing, Lyndie Gibson, Mags Gibson, Claire Hamilton, Heather Holton,
Jayne Johnson, Gayle McFedries, Emma McGhee, Dione McGregor, Sumi Mohammed,
Deborah Waite, Audrey Yildirim and Emma Richardson
who collaborated with me on the text for this book.

Text and illustrations © 2013 by Alison Murray

First U.S. edition, 2013
10 9 8 7 6 5 4 3 2
R969-8180-0-13309
Printed in China

Library of Congress Cataloging-in-Publication Data

Murray, Alison, M.A.
    Little mouse / Alison Murray.—1st U.S. ed.
        p. cm.
    Summary: A little girl explains how she does not always fit her nickname, little mouse,
but it is perfect for when she is cuddling with her mother.
    ISBN 978-1-4231-4330-7
    [1. Nicknames—Fiction. 2. Mother and child—Fiction.] I. Title.
PZ7.M95674Lit 2013
[E]—dc23   2012006147

Reinforced binding
Visit www.disneyhyperionbooks.com

Little Mouse

Alison Murray

Disney • Hyperion Books
New York

Sometimes,
when I'm being very
quiet and cuddly,
my mommy calls me her
little mouse.

But that's funny because I'm not little like a mouse—

I'm tall!

And I am actually very **strong.**

A little mouse nibbles its food,
but I chomp like a
hungry horse!

And I'm not timid like a little mouse...

I'm **very** brave . . .

... and I can be
scary too!

grrrr**RRRr**rr!

I don't really sound like
a little mouse...

Trumpety,
trump,
trump!

Too-wit, too-wit, too-woOOo!

yowly, hOwly, hOwl!

Squeak!

Oops!
That was a hiccup!

A little mouse
can't fly...

but I can **zoom high** into the **sky!**

"Bath time!"

And I'm pretty certain that little mice don't

stomp . . .

or waddle...

...or splash!

But just now,
right at this very moment,

I think I'm happy to be . . .

. . . quiet and cozy,

cuddly and dozy . . .

Mommy's
little
mouse.